Pig Kahuna

PiRATES!

Jennifer Sattler

BLOOMSBURY

NEW YORK   LONDON   NEW DELHI   SYDNEY

First published in the United States of America in April 2014
by Bloomsbury Children's Books
www.bloomsbury.com

For information about permission to reproduce selections from this book, write to
Permissions, Bloomsbury Children's Books, 1385 Broadway, New York, New York 10018
Bloomsbury books may be purchased for business or promotional use. For information on bulk purchases
please contact Macmillan Corporate and Premium Sales Department at specialmarkets@macmillan.com

Library of Congress Cataloging-in-Publication Data
available upon request
ISBN 978-1-61963-200-4 (hardcover) • ISBN 978-1-61963-201-1 (reinforced)

Art created with acrylics and colored pencil
Typeset in Birdlegs
Book design by Nicole Gastonguay

Printed in China by C&C Offset Printing Co., Ltd., Shenzhen, Guangdong
2 4 6 8 10 9 7 5 3 1 (hardcover)
2 4 6 8 10 9 7 5 3 1 (reinforced)

All papers used by Bloomsbury Publishing, Inc., are natural, recyclable products
made from wood grown in well-managed forests. The manufacturing processes
conform to the environmental regulations of the country of origin.

For Bob Barnes

It was Sunday. Dink had just woken up from his nap, grumpy and all out of sorts.

His big brother, Fergus,
suggested they go for a dip.

But it was *t-t-too c-c-cold*!

Fergus had another idea. "How about some castle building?"

Dink tried, but every
time he got started,
a mean ol' wave would
wash his castle away.

Usually a snack and a juice box
made Dink one happy little piglet.

But not today.

"Fergus! Your digging ruined my snack!"
Dink said, spitting out sand from his mouth.

He was so upset he threw his juice box.

"Dink!" cried Fergus. "This hole is not a trash can."

"Well," Dink answered, pointing, "what's THAT, then?"

A pirate hat!

Fergus was inspired.

He got right to work building a pirate ship out of sand.

Dink thought it looked like fun.

But he didn't really know
how to help.

As the ship got better
and better . . .

It's hard to build a pirate
ship when you're having
a temper tantrum.

It's also hard to
finish your snack.

Or take a walk.

And when a crab snapped
him on the toe . . .

"Shiver me timbers!" yelled Fergus.

"You're a perfect pirate,
Dink! You even have the
stink eye!"

"I am?" asked Dink. "I do?"
Fergus nodded.

He placed the pirate hat on Dink's head.

The two brothers took their places onboard the ship.

Fergus saluted, shouting,
"I saw a sea monster
headed that way, Captain!"

"Aaarrrgh!"